THE SONG AT THE SCAFFOLD

GERTRUD VON LE FORT

The Song at the Scaffold

Translated from the German
by Olga Marx

IGNATIUS PRESS   SAN FRANCISCO

Original German edition:
Die Letzte am Schafott
© 1931 by Kösel and Pustet, Munich

Previous English edition © 1933 by Sheed & Ward, Inc.
Reprinted with permission from
Deutsches Literaturarchiv, Marbach, Germany

Cover art by Stephen Dudro

Cover design by Riz Boncan Marsella

Reprinted in 2011 by Ignatius Press, San Francisco
All rights reserved
ISBN 978-1-58617-525-2
Library of Congress Control Number 2011926406
Printed in the United States of America ∞

I am Thine, I was born for Thee,
What is Thy will with me?
Let me be rich or beggared,
Exulting or repining,
And comforted or lonely!
O Life!—O Sunlight shining
In stainless purity!
Since I am Thine, Thine only,
What is Thy will with me?

"Hymn of Saint Teresa of Avila"
(*From the Spanish*)

Preface

he outbreak of the French Revolution led to wholly unexpected manifestations of hatred for the Christian faith. During the space of a few months, veritable throngs of priests and religious were led to the guillotine and executed. Among the victims were sixteen Carmelites belonging to a convent in Compiègne which had enjoyed special favors under the old régime. The present story is based upon their history and legend. It has been written in the form of a letter purporting to come from an observer of events in Paris to a noblewoman living in exile. The correspondents are familiar with the philosophical tendencies which flourished prior to the Revolution, and these are commented upon by the writer. While it will be easy for the reader to follow the progress of the narrative, some introductory remarks of a general character may not be taken amiss.

First, a word concerning the Carmel. Everyone had heard of this community, to which Saints as well-known and as different as Teresa of Avila and Thérèse of Lisieux have belonged. The sisters who elect to live according to the difficult Carmelite rule devote their lives to contemplative prayer and in particular to acts of expiation for evil done by other persons living in the world. Indeed the Carmelites have often been known to think of their community as a kind of "spiritual lightning rod", down which what would otherwise be wrathful flames of retribution pass harmlessly. Cloistered from the world and publicly engaged in no active tasks, these sisters are likely to be treated with malicious contempt in ages weak in faith.

And such was the period immediately preceding the French Revolution. Fraülein Gertrud von le Fort, the keenness of whose intuitive insight into religious psychology was appreciated by such a master as Ernst Troeltsch, presents in Sister Marie de l'Incarnation a woman possessing virtues which the time in which she lived almost completely lacked —nobility of soul, in which were fused both ability to govern and tactful knowledge of how to govern; and profound, clear, unshrinking faith, to which God was always the most self-evident of beings. To observe the outline of this Sister's character as it is here traced by an imagined contemporary is to share in one of the greatest pleasures art can afford— contemplation of the human in genuinely heroic form.

Nevertheless there is a sense in which such contemplation cannot suffice for the modern mind. Our current study of psychology, which in a way is also the recovery of knowledge which rationalistic psychologists mistakenly crowded out of their formulæ, is persistently aware of the universal mysteries hinted at in our own and others' subconscious minds.

We do not, should not, renounce heroism; but every great soul is only a pillar, however magnificently tall, and based upon discernible but never entirely measurable foundations of spiritual experience and purpose. All this is of special importance from the point of view of religious psychology. Here the center is forever God, never man. The valiant human soul thinks (too easily) that it sees all, comprehends us, can do all. Yet the Eternal Cosmos has a knowledge, a vision, a teleology which eddies round the isolated and so self-conscious individual as does the sea about a single ship. Therefore the life of Blanche has a peculiar significance. The Divine purpose, we seem to understand, could not have been achieved without the service of the weakness of fear. A timid girl seeks refuge in flight, and out of that running away come victory and unforgettable beauty. Did not the Lord's final redemptive achievement depend upon His leaning against a broken stave, and upon His coronation with a fool's garland?

The artist's gaze here scans deeps and heights. Nevertheless she does not content herself with unintelligible jottings—the shorthand of one who has strayed into the land of vision without the gift of sight. Everything is limpid, everything composed. This again is quite as it should be. The narrator etches by the steady light of his own illumination. He sees two worlds in conflict:—the human, which the philosophers had overestimated and which had again been broken, as in Greek myth, by its own aspirations; and the Divine, wherein man is always clay in the Potter's hands,

9

sometimes breathtakingly lustrous. *Quod semper, quod ubique.* This is a story of the French Revolution. It is also a vision of our own age, in which the spear of heedless, irreverent adventure has once more splintered against the wall.

G. N. S.

THE SONG AT THE SCAFFOLD

Chapter One

Paris, October 1794

n your letter to me, my dear friend, you emphasize the extraordinarily brave attitude with which women, the so-called weaker sex, face death every day of these terrible times. And you are right. With admiration you cite the poise of "noble" Madame Roland, of "queenly" Marie-Antoinette, of "wonderful" Charlotte Corday and "heroic" Mademoiselle de Sombreuil. (I am quoting your own adjectives.) You conclude with the touching sacrifice of the sixteen Carmelite nuns of Compiègne who mounted the guillotine singing *Veni Creator*; and you also mention the poignant and steadfast voice of young Blanche de la Force who finished the hymn that the executioner's knife silenced on the lips of her companions. "How nobly", you say toward the end of your eloquent letter, "the dignity of man triumphs in all these martyrs of the kingdom, of the Gironde and of the persecuted Church, martyrs caught in the waves of devastating chaos."

O dear disciple of Rousseau! As always I admire your

cheerful and noble faith in the indestructible nobility of human nature even when mankind is tasting most desolate failure. But chaos is nature too, my friend, the executioner of your women martyrs, the beast in man, fear and terror— all these are nature too! Since I am far closer to the frightful happenings in Paris than you, who have emigrated, permit me to confess candidly that I interpret the amazing resignation of those who die every day, less as an inherent natural grace than as the last supreme effort of a vanishing culture. Ah, yes! you despise culture, my dear friend, but we have learned to appreciate its value again, to respect conventional forms which prescribe restraint even to mortal terror and— in a few cases—something quite different.

Blanche de la Force was the last on your list of heroines. And yet she was not a heroine in your sense of the word. She was not elected to demonstrate the nobility of mankind but rather to prove the infinite frailty of all our vaunted powers. Sister Marie de l'Incarnation, the only surviving nun of Compiègne, confirmed me in this idea.

But, perhaps you do not even know that Blanche de la Force was a former nun of Compiègne? She was a novice there for a considerable period of time. Let me tell you a little of this exceedingly important episode in her life! For I believe it is the beginning of the famous song at the foot of the scaffold.

You know the Marquis de la Force, Blanche's father. So I need not tell you of his esteem for the skeptical writings of Voltaire and Diderot. You have heard of his sympathy for certain liberal patriots of the Palais Royal. His trends were purely theoretical and he never dreamed of concrete results. This sophisticated aristocrat did not think that the subtle spice of his conversation would ever season the crude cookery of the people. But let us not criticize the sad errors of our poor friend, for he, like so many others, has atoned for them. (Ah! my friend, when all is said and done, most of us were very like him.) Here we are only concerned with the motive that could induce a man like the Marquis de la Force to entrust his daughter to a convent.

While Blanche was in Compiègne, I spoke to her father on a few occasions in the cafés of the Palais Royal where he was rhapsodizing about liberty and fraternity with similarly minded friends. Whenever anyone asked him about his daughter he answered ruefully that he considered "the prisons of religion"—this was his name for convents—as undesirable as those of the state. Nevertheless he was forced to admit that his daughter felt happy there, happy and safe. "Poor timid child," he usually added, "the sad circumstances of her birth apparently determined her whole attitude toward life." And this, indeed, was the common view of the matter.

You, my dear friend, will scarcely understand the Marquis' allusion, because at the time he has reference to, you yourself were still a child. He was speaking of the notorious fireworks catastrophe at the wedding of Louis the Sixteenth, then a dauphin, with the daughter of the emperor of Austria.

Later this catastrophe was regarded as an evil omen that

foreshadowed the fate of the royal pair. Well, perhaps it was not merely an omen but also a symbol of fate. (For revolutions are caused and conditioned, to be sure, by mismanagement and mistakes in the existing system. But their essential character is the violent outbreak of the deadly fear of an epoch approaching its end. And it is this I had in mind when I spoke of a symbol.)

For it is not at all true that neglect on the part of the authorities was responsible for the unfortunate accident on the square of Louis the Fifteenth. This rumor was spread by people who wished to delude themselves about the mystery of that sudden and violent terror of the masses. Mystery, as you know, is intolerably annoying to enlightenment such as ours! As a matter of fact, the authorities were at their post. All the usual precautions had been taken with model efficiency. The carriages of the nobility, and among them the conveyance of the young Marquise de la Force, who was an expectant mother, were greeted respectfully by the crowd of pedestrians near the heavy water wagons of the *pompiers*, which were conscientiously held in readiness for all emergencies. Police officers stood at the intersections of the streets which ran into the square, and kept order. In spite of the "wretched times", which were almost proverbial, people looked well-dressed and well-fed. Practically every individual represented a well-to-do burgher of decent thinking and behavior. It was difficult to imagine them as part of the anarchistic chaos of half an hour later. For they were full of eager anticipation of a festive spectacle and responded to the police in orderly fashion. In short, the dreadful incident which followed was sudden and inexplicable. For it was an omen.

A harmless little blaze in the room where the fireworks were stored, and wild and instant panic, although there was absolutely no danger, caused mad confusion. At the street corner the policemen were unable to make a gesture—for they had disappeared! The happy and loyal citizens had disappeared. There remained only a wild monster, a mass of human beings stifled by their own terror: it was chaos that slumbers in the depths of all things and breaks through the solid armor of habit and custom.]

Through the windows of her fine carriage, in the midst of that fearful throng, the Marquise saw a gruesome spectacle. She heard the despairing cries of those who had fallen to the ground, she heard the groans of trodden bodies. But she herself was as safe in her great coach as if she had been on a ship secure on storm-tossed seas. Involuntarily she put out her slender, aristocratic hand and bolted the door. The bolt was a little rusty because the coach hailed from the time of the Fronde, when all carriage doors had been supplied with bolts since one never knew when there might be occasion for flight. But these bolts had not been used for a long time! The Marquise felt quite safe though she was considerably disturbed. This is not surprising for the sight of a crowd is always painful to the individual. Now whether the horses, confused by the noise and the turmoil, began to run of themselves, or whether the coachman lost his head and tried to escape, at any rate the coach began to move and drove straight into the screaming, raging, despairing crowd.

17

Almost at once the horses were stopped and the carriage door forced open. Seething chaos followed. For a moment there was something that resembled the revolution to come.

"Madame!" shrieked a man who bore a bloodstained child in his arms, "you are safe and secure in your coach while the people are dying under the hooves of your horses! But soon, I tell you, it is you who will be dying and we shall sit in your coaches." And even as he spoke the Marquise saw his menacing expression mirrored in hundreds of terror-stricken faces. In another moment she had been dragged from her carriage and her own expression of fear merged with that of the mass.

Rumor had it later that Blanche de la Force was born in the half-wrecked carriage on the way home from the square. This is an exaggeration. But it is true that the Marquise arrived at her palace on foot with torn garments and the face of a Medusa, and that, as the result of her terrible experience, she was confined prematurely and died soon afterward.

Now I do not hesitate to associate the temperament of the poor child with the circumstances of her birth. Not only the superstition of the people but the opinion of qualified physicians consider such a connection quite possible. Blanche, thrust into the world too soon through the fright of her mother, seemed to have been dowered only with fear. At an early age she displayed a timidity which greatly exceeded the little fears one usually observes in children. (Children are afraid of all sorts of things and one is apt to consider this a lack of understanding.) If her own little dog barked suddenly, she trembled; and she recoiled from the face of a new servant as though he were a ghost. It was impossible to cure her of fearing a niche in the passage which she passed every day with her nurse. At the sight of a dead bird or snail in the garden she froze to a statue. It seemed as if this pathetic little person lived in constant expectation of some shocking event which she might perhaps avoid by eternal watchfulness like that of small sick creatures who sleep with open eyes; or as if the great fear in her childish gaze penetrated the firm exterior of a sheltered life to a core of terrible frailty.

"Are you sure the stairs will not slip from under my feet?" she inquired when she was taken to the solid tower of the Château la Force, the ancestral home of her race, where the Marquis spent the summer. This tower had already defied seven centuries and everyone could see that it was capable of lasting seven more. "Won't the wall tip over? Are you sure the gondola will not sink? Won't people get angry?" This was the kind of thing little Blanche was constantly asking. And there was no use explaining to her that there was no cause for alarm. She would listen attentively and reflect on everything she was told, for she was by no means unintelligent, but she continued to be afraid. Neither affection nor severity nor her own indubitable willingness to improve, altered her unfortunate temperament. Indeed her very willingness made matters worse for she became so depressed by the futility of her efforts that she considered the lack of that courage which everyone urged upon her as the most shameful disgrace. One might almost say that in addition to everything else she grew to be afraid of her own fear. I have said that Blanche was not unintelligent; she had a good mind and so in time she invented little devices to mask the true state of affairs. She no longer asked: "Won't the stairs slip from under me?" or, "Are you sure the gondola will not sink?" But she would suddenly feel tired or ill, she had forgotten to learn her lesson or to fetch something she needed. In short there was some reason or other why she could not set foot on the stairs or in the gondola.

The servants laughed and dubbed her "rabbit-heart" but she did not improve, she even suffered more than formerly from her weakness because now she was trying to hide it. Sometimes one could see the agonies she was enduring. Never before had there been a comely child of noble birth who moved with such awkward timidity, who blushed so unfortunately as Blanche de la Force. The great title of her family was like a placard she bore unrightfully; the proud name of de la Force was idle mockery. No one who remembered her little face that paled so easily could call her anything but just Blanche. But "rabbit" was after all the most suitable name of all. This was the state of affairs when the Marquis de la Force engaged Madame de Chalais.

This excellent governess undertook Blanche's religious instruction with decision and thoroughness and by this approach succeeded in overcoming the child's fears to a certain extent. For because of the liberal tendencies of the Marquis, this aspect of her education had been deplorably neglected up to this time, and since Blanche, unlike her father, had the pronounced needs of a religious nature, the omission must have been especially fatal for her.

From a psychological point of view Madame de Chalais

was probably wise in directing her young pupil's attention to the Christ Child before everything else. It was Blanche's first encounter with "*le petit Roi de Gloire.*" (You, my dear friend, are acquainted with this charming little wax figure of the Carmelite convent in Compiègne, a figure that delighted the children at Christmas time when it was exhibited in the chapel.)

Le petit Roi had a crown and a scepter of gold which the King of France had given Him to show that *le petit Roi* was the ruler of Heaven and earth. In gratitude for his gift, *le petit Roi* protected the King and his people: and so it was quite possible to live safely in France without having to think of slipping stairs and tottering walls. Only, of course, one must give due reverence to *le petit Roi*, just as the King always did. One could do this without bestowing crowns and scepters, by prayers and little acts of love, obedience and worship. If one was conscientious in all these things one might depend upon the protection of *le petit Roi* as confidently as the King of France himself. Well, I have told you that Blanche had a religious nature and yet in the beginning Madame de Chalais met with unexpected obstacles. In later years she preferred to keep silence on that score, although as a rule she liked to indulge in reminiscences of her educational methods.

"Surely you must see how easy it is for the King of Heaven to protect you", she once said to Blanche in her gentle obstinate way when the child was again hesitating to go upstairs. "Only think of the great power of even our own king on earth!"

Blanche lifted her troubled little face to her governess.

21

Sometimes her tremulous glances resembled flocks of restless birds. "But if He lost His crown?" she asked pensively.

For a moment Madame de Chalais was nonplussed. It was true that this objection had never occurred to her. But almost instantly she rejected it—she was very apt in rejecting uncomfortable questions. Blanche sometimes imagined that they rebounded from the whalebones of her bodice which was a little too tight for her.

"You cannot believe in all seriousness, Blanche," she said, "that one loses one's crown as easily as a handkerchief. But one must have the proper respect for it! You promised me never to omit your prayer, and so you may rest assured that the King of Heaven will never fail to protect you. You can really go up the stairs without worrying."

Blanche quailed. It was the very stairway about which she had always asked whether it would slip from her. Involuntarily she freed her hand from the clasp of her governess and groped for one of the supports of the banister. And Fate had it that the support broke!

The little frightened birds in Blanche's eyes fluttered to Madame de Chalais in terror. For a moment fear and security regarded each other almost with hostility. Then it suddenly seemed as if not the stairs but Madame de Chalais slipped, as though she had assumed the rôle of the child.

"How can you frighten me so?" she cried. And she recoiled a little so that the bones of her tight bodice crackled softly.

Of course this mood did not last long. Madame de Chalais

was not accustomed to yield to moods. And, as I have already said, Blanche's resistance weakened at that time when the ideas and symbols of Christian piety were crowding out the uncertain phantasies of fear from her imagination. I can quite understand this. Ah, my friend, what consolation there is in faith! From my own childhood days I remember the strange penetration of prayer through all the layers of being down to the very foundation of all things where falling is possible no longer. Undoubtedly Blanche must have had similar sensations. The poor child who had stubbornly refused all earthly guarantees of safety began to confide her little anxious heart to the shelter of the Supreme Power. The little rabbit took courage. Madame de Chalais even had the satisfaction of seeing her smile at her own former fears and of mocking them in mischievous jests that savored a little of youthful boasting but satisfied everyone nevertheless.

She was sixteen now, slender, with a small delicate mouth and a face that looked a little peaked and strained. Madame de Chalais had been careful to accustom her to a bodice as tight as her own, and so the girl's movements were graceful but somewhat constrained. No one, however, would have called her shy. Since everything had turned out so favorably, the Marquis de la Force set about planning a suitable marriage for his daughter. But Madame de Chalais surprised him with the information that Blanche did not wish to marry, but that she desired to become a nun.

❧

Chapter Two

ow you can easily imagine that a man like the Marquis de la Force, who agreed with the most brilliant intellects in France that the Church was an institution of the past, raised objections. His friends heard him remark in high ill-humor that he had set his hopes upon Madame de Chalais and that all she had done after all was to build for Blanche a bridge by which the child could conveniently quit this world. She was just as fearful as ever, most likely! And the Marquis reasoned that for certain natures the vast confusion of life ends in the convent where definite boundaries are set to the welter of possibilities, where Destiny offers no unanticipated challenge or violence, where life moves amid firm-fixed regulations and thoughts and walls. And the latter, so the Marquis expressed himself, did not open upon reality but only to the pleasant illusion of Heaven and its inhabitants.

Now although his train of thought was certainly distorted, he was faintly right as far as Blanche's decision was concerned. But it would have been most unjust to the young girl to weigh only such considerations! We must repeat again and again that Blanche was really religious. In Carmel de Compiègne, where Madame de Chalais had connections, she made the very best impression. When she was introduced to the Prioress—at that time the invalid Prioress Croissy was still living—she answered the question as to whether she did not fear the severe regulations of the convent with the tinge of boastfulness she now displayed in matters of courage: "Oh, Reverend Mother, truly there are other things to be feared more than these slight sacrifices!"

Thereupon the Prioress (whom Madame de Chalais had told of Blanche's former difficulties) took occasion to ask her of what, for instance, she would be afraid.

Blanche reflected for a moment. Then she answered less positively than at first:

"I do not know, Holy Mother, but if you bid me, I shall think about it and answer you later."

"I do not bid you", Madame de Croissy replied quickly. She was still young at that time but already marked by the wasting disease of which she died soon after. They say that God put upon her a great dread of death some time before she died (it was then that she prayed so often in the convent garden and that therefore she felt sympathy for Blanche). As a matter of fact it is not altogether usual that a religious order as severe as that of the Carmelites should have admitted so frail a young girl.

So Blanche de la Force entered upon her enclosure and we are told that her strained little face shone with such fervent happiness that everyone in Carmel de Compiègne was convinced of her vocation and believed that she would become a worthy daughter of Saint Teresa.

She was a satisfactory postulant. It was not altogether easy for her to observe the strict regulations of the order—still she observed them. She was amiable, eager, obedient, and—this must be emphasized particularly—she was happy and grateful too. This was especially pronounced when disquieting rumors crossed the threshold of the convent. And that was hardly avoidable in those times. (It was shortly before the summoning of the Estates General.) We are told that on such occasions Blanche's expression was one of indescribable contentment, that she even clapped her hands childishly and exclaimed with a trace of gay arrogance, "That does not concern us here." Or, "It won't reach us! We are safe here."

Just as she had once repeated the easy maxims of Madame de Chalais, so now she adopted certain heroic locutions in the style of the Carmelites, "O God, to Thee do I sacrifice myself completely!" Or, "O Suffering, sweet peace to the lovers of God, may I learn to know thee!" But gradually the words she had learned to repeat so effortlessly had their effect upon her—and certain reactions took place.

This became particularly evident when, at about this time, the Prioress Croissy died. Her death struggle was very painful. For hours the sound of her moaning filled the convent. Blanche was bewildered and shocked and asked how it was possible that God permitted so holy a woman to suffer so. She exhibited such horror and apprehension that the whole convent was amazed. Indeed, her investiture was postponed at the time because Sister Marie de l'Incarnation, the novice mistress, was seized with doubt. But in the end it took place quite suddenly.

It was the year seventeen hundred and eighty-nine and the national assembly convening at Versailles was taking action against church property as a relief measure for the financial depression of the country. (You will probably recall the decision I have in mind.)

Already that summer the superior of the Carmelite Order, Monsignore Rigaud, had informed the convents under his jurisdiction that a law which forbade the admission of new members was pending. Monsignore did not hesitate to disclose that the national assembly was contemplating the complete suppression of religious orders. But there was hope, he said, that the law might be altered to permit those who were already members to remain so, and to allow them to die out. In consideration of these circumstances Monsignore advised the immediate investiture of postulants unless there were some special individual objection. This wise and liberal prelate wrote: "Let us confide these young girls to the guidance of God unless there are unambiguous reasons against such a procedure, and let us not be petty but liberal in regard to them. For in time to come, God himself will choose and distinguish between them. Christ", so the letter concluded, "may be said to be in the garden of Gethsemane. I therefore recommend the name of Jésus au Jardin de l'Agonie for the postulants since under the conditions prevailing today no more suitable name could be found." (You know, my friend, that in Carmelite convents they believe that the religious name the individual Sister receives at her investiture gives her special access to the mystery expressed by that name.)

Under these circumstances the newly elected prioress, Madame Lidoine (her religious name was Sister Theresa of Saint Augustin), thought it advisable to confer about Blanche with the novice mistress, Sister Marie de l'Incarnation.

But let us learn the upshot of this discussion from Sister Marie de l'Incarnation herself or, as the children of the charming singer Rose Ducor called her, Sister Marie of the Christchild, for that is how their mother had explained the unintelligible name of de l'Incarnation to them.

You know, my friend, how this singer surprised us in the days of the revolution! In the world of the theater she was a veritable little goddess and some of her more frivolous admirers had accused her of coquetting with religion. But during the Reign of Terror she sheltered various priests and members of religious orders in her own home protected by her immense popularity. (Ah, my dear friend, people frequently surprise us by their steadfastness in the face of martyrdom. I shall never dare to express any positive views on these matters.) For a time Marie de l'Incarnation enjoyed the hospitality of Rose Ducor and her escape from the revolutionary tribunal is undoubtedly due to the calm presence of mind of the little singer.

Chapter Three

n those days I had the honor of calling on that distinguished nun on several occasions. She was engaged in writing a biography of her martyred Sisters. I found her seated at Madame Ducor's graceful desk of rosewood, arranging all sorts of papers. Of course she wore neither her robe nor her veil but was dressed in lay clothing, a bonnet on her head and her kerchief drawn so closely around her neck that it covered the place where obstinate rumor had insisted she bore a narrow red scar since the execution of her Sisters. Even the brave little singer likes to repeat this touching legend for she considers Marie de l'Incarnation a saint.

When she noticed that I was looking at her kerchief she pushed it aside with a sad and tremulous gesture but without a trace of resentment. And I ascertained, as doubtlessly she wished me to, that the rumor was false. But I understood why it had spread. For this woman really had a most impressive personality. It was easy and natural to believe miracles of her. (When one knows her nothing is more amazing than the touching name, "Sister Marie of the Christchild!") She might have served as a model for the statue of a saintly queen, even of a saintly king. So, at least, it seemed to me, and I do not think that this feeling was based only on the knowledge of her origin. You must know, my friend, that this Sister is supposed to be the natural daughter of a French prince. Up to the time of the revolution she actually received an income from the state; and it is known that because of her illegitimate birth she required a special dispensation from the bishop to enable her to enter the convent of Carmel. They say that as a young girl she lived in brilliant circumstances and then quite suddenly, at the grave of the Carmelite nun, Madame Acarie, she was seized by a burning desire to expiate the sins of the court (to which she owed her life!), just as Madame Louise de France, the prioress of Carmel de Saint Denis, had done before her. This past history of hers explains a great deal in the life of this rare and noble soul. Well—I stated my question concerning Blanche de la Force.

She gave me a most peculiar answer. It was really another question. "Must fear and horror always be evil? Is it not possible that they may be deeper than courage, something that corresponds far more to the reality of things, to the terrors of the world, and to our own weakness?"

I was greatly astonished at her words for you know, dear friend, that it was Sister Marie de l'Incarnation who persuaded the convent of Carmel de Compiègne to offer Heaven that heroic consecration, which, in a way, foreshadowed the fate of the convent. (I shall speak of that in a moment.)

"So fear is deeper than courage—and you say this, Sister Marie de l'Incarnation?" I asked.

She ignored my allusion to her heroism and went back to my first question.

"As a matter of fact," she said, "there were those among us who approved of Blanche's return to the world. But our Reverend Mother, the Prioress Lidoine of St. Augustin, decided otherwise. Madame Lidoine had the greatest wisdom and knowledge of souls."

"And yet", I replied, "the results have proved that Madame Lidoine was wrong." (I was thinking of Blanche's flight from Compiègne.)

"Not Madame Lidoine," she replied quickly, "but another Sister. For you must know that not all of us understood fully the guidance of our Reverend Mother."

Suddenly I had the unerring though inexplicable conviction that she was speaking of herself. At the same moment she looked at me and I colored under her gaze. She herself remained quite unconcerned.

A brief silence ensued, filled with unspoken thoughts. At last she said, with a strange childlike expression so oddly in contrast with her proud clear-cut features that I was almost confused: "And why should you not know it, Monsieur de Villeroi? Have you not come to learn the truth? I assure you that this truth will glorify His Majesty more than any other!" (For in the convent of Carmel they designate God as His Majesty.)

Then she gave me various documents. Some were notes of the Prioress Lidoine, notes that constituted a sort of journal of her office. And some were written in her own hand, for, as I have already said, she was working at a biography of the martyred Sisters.

I shall draw upon these two manuscripts and relate whatever is of importance to us.

Sister Marie de l'Incarnation urged the Reverend Mother not to permit Blanche's investiture and pointed to her peculiar weakness of fear.

"O Reverend Mother," she said and her beautiful spirited eyes rested upon the Prioress (she could not look up to her since she was considerably taller), "this poor child moves me to compassion for she has sought shelter in the walls of the convent as a bird slips into the nest. I do not love this child less because she is weak. But just because I love her!—O Reverend Mother, the world is so full of little pieties, there are hundreds of these tiny flames! Every day they burn before countless altars of Paris and hosts upon hosts are blown out by the storms of life. Such little flames do not belong in a convent! The Carmelites demand absolute strength and faith!"

Let me interrupt my tale for a moment. I have just described the impression which the personality of Marie de l'Incarnation made upon me, but perhaps I should tell you a little about her position in the convent and above all of her attitude toward the new prioress.

Madame Lidoine undoubtedly esteemed her highly for in her journal she calls her her "right hand", her "daughter adviser", once even her "motherly daughter". And she mentions that after the death of the Prioress Croissy, she had hoped that Sister Marie de l'Incarnation would be chosen in her place. But that the Church had selected a "far lesser one." By this she meant herself!

"It is true that Madame Lidoine was quite insignificant both in appearance and in her religious life. This was especially evident in the period following her election. It was very difficult for her to acquire the habit of giving commands to those she considered above her, and so she gave the false impression of being uncertain." So said Sister Marie de l'Incarnation and she added: "This apparent wavering was a great temptation to me." (So she herself broached the sore spot of her relationship to the Prioress for there is no doubt that she dominated her.)

In this matter also the Reverend Mother did not actually contradict her. She merely handed her the letter of Monsignore.

Marie de l'Incarnation read it. Her expressive face changed. She blushed and paled. One could see how greatly this communication of the restriction of membership in the order affected her. When she had finished she said with deep emotion: "What a difficult choice, Reverend Mother!"

Madame Lidoine had evidently expected a different answer. She looked shy and timid as always when she had to oppose Marie de l'Incarnation.

"Do you think it is a question of choice?" she asked in her deep voice. (This voice was the most characteristic thing about her.) Marie de l'Incarnation answered quickly —she had the utmost sensitiveness and subtlety of perception: "You desire this investiture, Reverend Mother?"

35

"Monsignore wishes it", the Prioress answered almost apologetically.

Marie de l'Incarnation submitted at once. (My dear friend, it is touching to follow the efforts of this great soul to attain complete humility.) "Under these conditions," she said, "I cannot, it is true, retract my opinion of our postulant, but I shall beg God to accept me as a sacrifice for her. Permit me, Reverend Mother, to assist the soul entrusted to our care by extraordinary acts of love and atonement, so that admission to our community may not endanger her in any way." (You know that in the Carmelite convents such acts of heroic love can be accomplished by one Sister for another, and undoubtedly Madame Lidoine was happy to hear of Marie de l'Incarnation's pious decision.)

So the investiture of Blanche was decided upon. Now in the Carmel de Compiègne they knew with absolute certainty that this event would be the last of its kind for a long time to come, and so the ceremony was endowed with poignant significance. But we must not fancy that the majority of the Carmelite nuns were at all concerned or troubled. The members of this order, which is often termed somber because of the severity of its penances, are usually as carefree and merry as children. At this time everyone in Compiègne was happy that, notwithstanding difficult conditions, they were to succeed in admitting another young Sister to the order of Carmel. The little novice Constance de Saint Denis expressed quite naïvely the idea that may have prompted the counsel of Monsignore: "Dear little Sister Blanche," she said, "let us hold together, you and I, and play a trick on the national assembly! We are young, and though it is sad to contemplate that we shall reach Heaven so late, let us hope to grow a hundred years old. For by that time new novices will surely be admitted to our order again."

In the meantime Blanche in her brown habit and the white veil of the novice looked just as frail and appealing as when she had first gone into seclusion. Surreptitiously, her hands trembling with happiness, she would caress the rough wool of her robe, and this gesture was so eloquent of her state of mind that the convent felt at peace about her.

On the evening of the day of her investiture, Madame Lidoine wrote: "The gratitude of our young daughter is indescribable. For the poor child knew very well that her strength was failing and had not been prepared to receive the veil. 'Oh, how good is His Majesty! How good is the Reverend Mother! How kind Sister Marie de l'Incarnation!' Again and again she repeated these words. When she heard the name she was to bear from that time on, she shuddered a little, but her joy was so great that she soon regained her composure. During the recreation in the garden she suddenly and impulsively fell on her knees in the olive grove where the Prioress Croissy had knelt so often, and lifting her voice in deep fervor, she publicly accepted her new name by uttering this prayer: 'O Lord Jesus, in this garden of Gethsemane I yield myself utterly to Thee!'"

"Because of her humble gratitude and because of the name which Heaven gave to this timid child, I am full of hope", so Madame Lidoine concluded. "O Jesus in the Garden of Gethsemane, this is my prayer also, strengthen the spirit of

Thy young bride and send her a succoring angel such as attended Thee and gave Thee balm in Thy hour of mortal fear!"

And it actually seemed as if this time the hopes of the convent were to be fulfilled. They no longer suspected Blanche of simply repeating the heroic ritual of the Carmelite faith, nor did she seem to be oppressed by it. The young novice was as fervent as on the day of her reception and made such decided progress that even Sister Marie de l'Incarnation was satisfied. And because of this general confidence in Blanche her second relapse was all the more shocking.

But here I must give you a brief summary of events.

Chapter Four

I do not know whether at that time similar measures were taken in other convents and whether they were connected with recent investitures, but the fact remains that soon after Blanche had been received as a novice a commission arrived in Compiègne with the purpose of conducting investigations as to the number, the age, and the religious sincerity of the Sisters. For in those days the authorities already intended to persuade the members of religious orders to return to the world, that is to say, to annul their vows, and they naïvely expected the majority to throw themselves jubilantly into the arms of the triumphant Revolution.

Before the commission interviewed individual Sisters, it made a survey of the entire convent. According to reports I heard, I am under the impression that they suspected some concealment or other. For since the publication of Diderot's famous story, all our freethinkers were full of fairy tales about imprisoned nuns!

They went from cell to cell and Sister Marie de l'Incarnation accompanied them, in obedience to the command of the Reverend Mother. Probably these men did not walk very noisily, perhaps they even walked with that uncertainty which the representatives of a new order usually feel toward an old established culture. But they walked as men do walk (and remember that these corridors were accustomed to the hushed feet of women!). It is likely, too, that they did not wish to show any respect for their surroundings. (It is significant that the Choir Sisters had been forced to raise their veils.) The faces of the men must have expressed this lack of reverence but I do not believe that they could have been especially threatening, for they still hoped to bend the order to their wishes without the use of violence. Marie de l'Incarnation told me that even the most objectionable member of the commission, a bold little fellow who obviously held an inferior position, was comical rather than terrible as he trotted along in advance of the others, a red cap perched awry on his greasy hair, and flung open the doors of the cells. I am sure he felt a shameless delight in penetrating the enclosure of a convent. But as I have said, all this did not make him at all dreadful but merely contemptible and bizarre. And yet he affected poor Blanche with utter terror. For as soon as this absurd little fellow opened the door of her cell and peeped through the crack with a grin, she uttered a piercing scream. (Sister Marie de l'Incarnation told me that in the worst days of the subsequent revolution she never again heard such a cry.) At the same time she retreated toward the wall of her cell with outstretched hands as if she were warding off unspeakable horror and when she could go no further she stopped as if she were awaiting death.

The men stood still too, at first in surprise, and then with growing interest. Apparently they believed they had found the prisoner whose presence they had suspected. At any rate the leader began to speak to Blanche with the utmost affability and tried to persuade her to give him her confidence.

She was so terror-stricken that she could not reply. But when, encouraged by her silence, he suggested that perhaps she wished to leave the convent, a second terror broke the spell of the first and she burst into a flood of tears.

The fellow was delighted at the prospect of saving a victim of religion and displayed great eagerness in a good cause. He told her that she might consider herself entirely free, that the new laws permitted no more investitures. He was about to take her hand in a fatherly manner when Sister Marie de l'Incarnation intervened. Her beautiful eyes blazed at him in stern determination as she said: "Monsieur, you are exceeding your authority. As far as I know the law of which you speak has not yet become valid."

I do not know what his answer would have been if Blanche at that moment had not fled to the arms of her novice mistress and thus given him the clearest reply in the world. He saw that he had made a mistake and colored like a rejected suitor.

In the meantime the professed nuns stood grouped around their Prioress in the chapter room. Had she been taller one might have made the comparison of chickens clustered about the mother hen, but as it was, Madame Lidoine almost disappeared among her daughters.

One by one the Choir Sisters were called into the chapter room and to give more weight to the procedure, the entrances were guarded by soldiers. As she went, each Sister bade farewell to the Reverend Mother who counseled her to give brief but courteous answers, for such had been the advice of Monsignore Rigaud. Well, you can imagine that their replies indicated loyalty to the order. There were no difficulties of any kind. Only the interview with Marie de l'Incarnation was characterized by a short, stormy interlude.

It is my opinion that this would have occurred without the preceding episode in Blanche's cell. Imagine this tall distinguished woman of noble birth face to face with those proletarians! Picture to yourself a nun imbued with her mystic mission of atonement before those dry officials, and you will see that a clash was unavoidable, even if the way had not been paved for it. Of course, from a psychological point of view, the leader bore a grudge to this nun who had shamed him publicly. In his very first words he clearly revealed the desire to humiliate her by asking her contemptuously whether she and the la Force Sister had recovered from their attack of fear.

Marie de l'Incarnation knew that she had not been afraid but at this moment she felt a maternal and sisterly responsibility to protect the weakness of the poor little novice from outsiders. There is no doubt that she was seized with the desire to uphold the honor of the order which her young pupil had endangered and this explains the extraordinary boldness with which she faced the commission.

"What do you mean by the word fear, Monsieur?" she asked. "How can we fear anything but the thought of displeasing Christ, allegiance to whom you are giving us the honor to proclaim?''

This answer was, of course, calculated to increase the man's ill-suppressed anger. (It is always difficult for small souls to endure the profession of a faith alien to them.) Again he transgressed the limits of his power.

"You are mistaken, Citizeness", he replied. "We are not here to afford you the honor of listening to your fanatical profession but to ask you in the name of the nation whether or not you will leave this hotbed of superstition. But allow me to suggest to you that the representatives of the nation have authority so complete as to inspire a certain amount of that fear which you—wrongly, I believe—rejected just now!" Ah! the deluded man did not feel that this open hostility, instead of intimidating them, was kindling the fervor of these Carmelites. (For, my friend, Christianity thrives upon persecution and this is the reason why all brutality, crude or subtle, directed against it, becomes merely stupid.)

Marie de l'Incarnation divined the threat which a moment later she was to hail as a special honor conferred upon her.

"My profession of faith", she replied fearlessly, "contains my answer to your question. But as far as the authority of the representatives of the nation is concerned, it is only as great as God permits. Not an iota more! Let me tell you this, Monsieur!''

You can readily understand that these words added fuel to flame! "Very well," he replied, "I shall remember your answer. The movement afoot now is not yet at an end. I hope the day will come when churches and convents will

43

be besieged as well as the Bastille. But do you happen to know what happened to the commander of the Bastille, Citizeness?" (He was referring to De Launys whose head, dripping with blood, the people bore on a pike through the city!)

For a second she was completely silent and motionless. Doubtless the man was already enjoying the satisfaction of having frightened her to death. Then slowly a flush of happiness mounted to her face.

"I know", she answered softly. "Oh, I know very well!" It was as if her voice were kneeling overcome by strange ecstasy. She crossed her arms on her breast.

My friend, we must stop to examine that attitude of the Carmelites with which we are both fairly unfamiliar. It depends so utterly on the concept of sacrifice of one to save the many, that in them the Christian belief in salvation by the Cross is transmuted into a fervent love of suffering and persecution. I know that it is hard for the non-Christian world, even for the world at large, to comprehend this idea, that it may even be considered pathological. In spite of this, I beg you to suppress your own sense of values and to accept the Carmelite point of view simply as a matter necessary for the understanding of this story. (Or rather for the understanding of all Christianity.)

"When I left the chapter room," Marie de l'Incarnation told me, "I felt as if a tall, solemn funeral taper had been lit within me, and its light suffused me so that I seemed to become entirely transparent."

And at sight of her the Reverend Mother said at once:

44

"Why, you are aglow as an angel, my daughter. What has happened to you?"

She replied in a voice stifled by emotion. But her exultation broke through: "O Reverend Mother! Wish me joy! Wish us all joy! Felicitate this land and this throne! His Majesty will permit us to perform a penance we never dreamed of: they have threatened me with martyrdom!"

To her surprise Madame Lidoine did not seem to share her rapture. She only asked rather dryly how such an undesirable situation had come about.

Marie de l'Incarnation fell on her knees at once. She accused herself of having exceeded the commands of the Reverend Mother, of not having spoken with gentle brevity. "For", she told me, "at that time I had no lack of zeal to overcome my pride, but I had not fully recognized the seat of it." (The flaws in this great soul, my friend, lay so far beyond common shortcomings!)

And the Prioress replied at once, and I do not think that it was only because there were others in the room: "There was never any question of a command, my daughter, only of advice."

Chapter Five

eanwhile poor Blanche was still in a deplorable condition which I believe we may term a nervous breakdown. During this period, Sister Marie de l'Incarnation remained at the side of the young novice as her untiring nurse and companion. Now I fancy that the personality of this great nun must have been very suggestive and that the goal was reached the more easily since Blanche looked to her novice mistress with all the yearning admiration of the weak for the strong. And so, a few days later, she appeared again in the circle of the Sisters and was obviously concerned in atoning for the bad impression she had made in her interview with the commission. In the refectory, according to the custom of convents, she penitently accused herself of weakness and commended herself at the same time to the prayers of the Sisters. It was really astonishing that so much humility and good will did not prove to be more fruitful.

The outsider may say that it is not hard to understand that a young and somewhat delicate nun showed anxiety during the following period. For I remember quite well that at that time convents were robbed in various sections of the country. Such acts, indeed, were the natural response of the people to the decisions against the Church that had been made by the national assembly. Blanche had good reason to be concerned and she showed concern. She did not admit this voluntarily, but it could be recognized easily by little involuntary signs. When I consider the matter as a whole, I might even say that as far as Madame de Chalais' excellent education was concerned, a carefully wound-up ball of yarn was unwinding itself again. Or, to express it differently: the vanished little rabbit had returned and behaved exactly as it had years ago. As a child Blanche had asked continually whether the stairs would not slip from under her or whether people would not grow angry. And now, during the recreation, she would suddenly inquire in a small, agonized voice whether any new robberies had occurred or whether they would surely permit members of orders to remain in their convents.

"I am not at all afraid", she would say with a gallant gesture that was so pathetically false (and no one believed her little attempts at boasting any more), "no, I am really not afraid! What is there to be afraid of? If the King of France is powerful, how much more—" Here she was involuntarily repeating a phrase of Madame de Chalais' but suddenly she stopped, for she probably remembered how badly the King had fared recently when the people dragged him, a prisoner, from Versailles to Paris. The *Carmagnole* and the *Ça ira*, which sounded more and more often from the street into the convent garden, caused her discomfort too. She would suddenly ask the Prioress for permission to fetch a forgotten book—just as she had done as a child. She almost gave the impression that she wanted to hide somewhere, where she could not hear the singing.

"Dear little Sister Blanche, let's play a trick on the national assembly and grow to be a hundred years old", the young and naïve novice Constance Saint Denis said to her. "Let us survive all these horrid laws about convents. How can you spoil things for yourself by being so afraid?" And another time: "Are we not the brides of Christ?" And the old Sister Jeanne de l'Enfance de Jésus who was really almost a hundred years old, said: "Are we not servants of *le petit Roi de Gloire* and will He not give us strength and care for us under all conditions?" (The Carmelites did not say, as Madame de Chalais, "*Le petit Roi* will protect us", but they said, "He will give us strength"!)

At that time most of them lived in the same enthusiastic readiness as Marie de l'Incarnation, who now increased her prayers and her sacrifices for Blanche. (You recall, my friend, that she had pledged herself to do this before the too hurried reception of the young novice?) I have since hesitated to mention these sacrifices because I did not want to deprive them of their chief beauty—their complete secrecy. No one in Compiègne besides Madame Lidoine knew anything about them. Marie de l'Incarnation tried to conceal them from Blanche in particular. (In this curious nun we fathom new depths of religion again and again. She never tried to influence the novice entrusted to her care psychologically. She wished to work through sacrifice and prayer as she did in regard to the world itself, and to do this through God to whom she was offering her prayers. She knew only the ultimate in all things.)

In those days her influence in the community must have been extraordinary. I understand this: I really believe it would have been impossible for this woman to prevent her flaming urge to martyrdom from quickening others, even had she wished it. But she could not possibly wish it! Only remember the peculiar duty of her order, my friend! Do you recall how before the revolution the question would arise as to whether Christianity could still produce martyrs if the occasion presented itself? Later we learned the truth, namely that in this order martyrs were actually ready and waiting!

"France will not be saved by the zeal of its politicians but by the prayers and sacrifices of devoted souls! Today is the great hour of the Carmelite Order!" This was the chord to which the quiet Sisters of Compiègne were attuned in those days. They were deliberately preparing for martyrdom.

"Shall we really need these supplies?" asked the naïve little Constance de Saint Denis, when the Reverend Mother casually inquired whether vegetables necessary for the winter had been picked in the garden.

"Why should we not need these things, my child?" Madame Lidoine replied. Very often now she heard or rather overheard the question: "Shall we need this?" Among her nuns it was an open secret that she was strangely aloof from the heroic preparations of her daughters.

"The convent is stringing bright-colored beads", she says

jestingly in her journal, in regard to these preparations. And another time, "My daughters are again playing with the idea of martyrdom."

Now, my friend, I am far from wishing to belittle the heroic frame of mind of these pious women. And yet I must mention the fact that at that time there was no possible reason to believe in the probability of martyrdom. After all, the threats of an individual official were only a breach of manners in keeping with the impudence of the people. There were certain difficulties and limitations to be faced, perhaps a temporary dissolution of the order. But there was no dreadful issue at hand. Was it not a gross misinterpretation to accuse these humane times of bloodthirstiness? And was it not a little absurd to credit them with the awful crime of hating God, when in reality everyone was busy mouthing philosophical phrases and discussing pressing questions of state finance? At that time we did not think of subsequent developments. So heroism was really an extravagant figment of the fancy and as out of place as fear—if you will pardon me my frankness. And yet we would err in ascribing these considerations to Madame Lidoine's resistance to the behavior of the nuns.

You know, my friend, that the command which Monsignore had anticipated came very quickly. It categorically prohibited the reception of new novices and also forbade those already received to make their eternal vows. (Try to imagine the grief of a young Sister at this ruling which condemned her to an everlasting novitiate!) In the Carmelite convent of Compiègne, in addition to Blanche, Sister

Constance de Saint Denis was especially involved since she was shortly to take her vows.

At this juncture Marie de l'Incarnation emphatically recommended that she be permitted to do this in all secrecy, in the catacombs, as it were, just as Blanche had been received not so long ago.

"Is it so great a venture, Reverend Mother," she said to the Prioress with noble insistence, "is our daring so great, even if the matter is discovered? The sooner the world lets us feel its hatred, the better for that world!" (Do you observe here the slight change of attitude, the shift from mere readiness to the expressed wish? And you will, I believe, now understand Madame Lidoine's reluctance to share the enthusiasm of her daughters.)

At the time I was just speaking of, she surprised Marie de l'Incarnation by one of her first independent decisions. She rejected the suggestion with the somewhat depressing reason that on the occasion of Blanche's reception it had been the question of a prospective law, while now the ruling was in full force and she added that she did not think it advisable to rouse the anger of opponents needlessly.

This reason was of course not fundamental. I cannot resist describing to you how Madame Lidoine informed the two novices of the painful provisions of the new law. For here the veil of insignificance is raised from the soul of this woman who appeared so plain and usual to those about her. ("At that time", so Sister Marie de l'Incarnation told me, "she acted as a prioress for the first time and", she added softly, "in opposition to me!") Before she read the decree she prayed the famous hymn of her foundress Teresa of Avila, with her assembled daughters:

> I am Thine, I was born for Thee,
> What is Thy will with me?
> Let me be rich or beggared,
> Exulting or repining,
> And comforted or lonely!
> O Life!—O Sunlight shining
> In stainless purity!
> Since I am Thine, Thine only,
> What is Thy will with me?

Then she read the decree. "You, my daughters," she said to the two novices, "because of this cruel ruling will offer your vows to His Majesty by sacrificing the joy of pronouncing them openly. For it is not important", here the clear eyes of the Prioress fixed the Sisters, one after another, "to realize our own aims even though they may be most worthy, but to fulfill the wishes of God. Do not therefore rebel against this decree, my dear novices, but neither shall you try to suppress your sorrow by sheer force of will. Embrace your disappointment—and it is justifiable—in complete love of God, and you will be obeying the spirit of our order. You will be Carmelites in the full sense of the word at the very time when the world does not permit you to be Carmelites!"

Well, my friend, this speech and the prayer which preceded it, can be interpreted in many different ways. The only question is whether it was understood.

53

If Blanche understood it—and Madame Lidoine observed that she listened with rapt attention—her understanding bore no fruit. Indeed it must be admitted that just at this time her behavior began to be profoundly disturbing.

Chapter Six

t was Advent and the old Sister Jeanne de l'Enfance de Jésus was sewing a new shirt for *le petit Roi de Gloire*. It was turning out a little awry, for her eyesight was almost a hundred years old. But she had not wanted to give up this beloved duty.

"Dear little Sister Blanche, now they will soon bring our little King to you", she said to the young novice, "don't you feel a little happy about this?" (You know, my friend, that *le petit Roi de Gloire* is carried into the cell of every Carmelite on Christmas night. Blanche, who had just been received, was to experience this ceremony for the first time.)

Unfortunately a decree of the national assembly arrived a few days before the holiday. It confiscated all church goods and robbed *le petit Roi* of His crown and His scepter. Clad only in His poor little shirt, Madame Lidoine bore Him from cell to cell on Christmas night.

"Now our little King is as poor again as He was in Bethlehem", the Sisters said happily. These good and gentle women were tireless in their efforts to transmute all anguish into joy.

Blanche was moved. One saw it clearly on her face. Tears were in her eyes and two great drops fell on the little wax figure that was laid in her arms.

"So small and so weak", she murmured.

"No, so small and so powerful", whispered Sister Marie de l'Incarnation, who was standing beside her. She was not certain if Blanche had heard her. She was bending down to kiss *le petit Roi* and suddenly she noticed that He had no crown! At the same instant the wild strains of the *Carmagnole* rose from the street. Blanche started violently—*le petit Roi* fell from her hands and His little unprotected head struck the stone floor of the cell—and was severed from the body. "Oh, *le petit Roi* is dead", she cried. "Now there is only the living Christ!"

In the course of the night she must have gone through a dangerous crisis for when the Feast of the Holy Innocents was celebrated a few days later—and on this day it was the tradition for the youngest novice in the convent to rule all the rest—Constance de Saint Denis, who was two years older, had to take her place. But the worst of it was that Blanche suddenly gave the impression that she was no longer struggling against her condition as before. Up to now her ardent efforts to gain greater courage and poise had been reassuring to her superiors. But now it was sadly true that her resistance was lessening if not failing entirely! Marie de l'Incarnation was convinced that in some way or other she was accepting the situation.

This it seems was the reason why, in the convent of

Carmel de Compiègne, the advisability of urging the young novice to return to the world was duly weighed. For the novitiate is like a question which can be answered in the negative.

"My big daughter", so Madame Lidoine wrote at the time, "saw more clearly than I in this case. It will probably be necessary to retrace a false step as soon as possible. And", she adds, "poor Sister Marie de l'Incarnation! She had offered herself up entirely for this child. But His Majesty did not deign to accept the sacrifice."

She had Blanche summoned in order to tell her in person whatever she considered necessary.

Blanche came. Since the last crisis her face looked still smaller to the Prioress, even a little older, aged! If one can speak of age in the case of such extreme youth. And so her features, or rather the pinched, tormented expression of her features, seemed more apparent than usual. She must have divined why she had been called: she was like a little child that is to be punished; and yet at the same time there was about her a sense of being comforted, some final secret certainty and willingness.

The Prioress was touched with compassion when she saw her. "My child," she said gently, "I have a painful communication to make to you. But first let us together seek solace with God." She bade Blanche kneel with her. Then she prayed the hymn of Saint Teresa and asked Blanche to repeat it after her.

And now a strange thing happened. Blanche obeyed her at

once. With her small tortured voice that was almost breathless, she repeated the words said to her until she came to the place:

> "Let me be rich or beggared,
> Exulting or repining,—"

But at this point she continued:

> "And give me fear or refuge—
> Since I am Thine, Thine only,
> What is Thy will with me?"

She spoke very quickly, almost mechanically like one who says words one has known for a long time. She obviously did not realize that she was changing the text of the prayer. But the Prioress was keenly aware of it. At first she was about to correct Blanche but the same odd compassion she had felt before restrained her. Without touching upon Blanche's prayer she broached the subject at once.

"My child," she said, "I presume that you know why I had you called?"

Blanche was silent.

Madame Lidoine had not expected this silence. "I have always appreciated your humility", she continued, "and I am trusting this trait of yours to lighten this heavy hour for me, because this separation is no less painful for the mother than for the child." She embraced Blanche. But the silence was unbroken.

Madame Lidoine felt a slight embarrassment. "Do you think that I am doing you an injustice?" she asked a little uncertainly.

Blanche was silent.

Suddenly the Prioress said with unwonted haste: "I command you to speak, Sister Blanche! Am I or am I not doing you an injustice by sending you back into the world?"

Blanche knelt before her and covered her face with her hands. "You command me to speak, Reverend Mother", she said softly. "Well then, yes, you are doing me an injustice."

"Then your novice mistress is mistaken? You still hope to overcome your weakness?"

"No, Reverend Mother." There was something quite hopeless in her voice and at the same time a strange note of peace.

The Prioress felt as though suddenly all her standards were collapsing. "Look at me", she commanded. Blanche dropped her hands from her small tortured face that held only a single expression of endless depths. The Prioress hardly recognized her. A series of quite unconnected images suddenly floated before her: little dying birds, wounded soldiers on the battlefield, criminals at the gallows. She seemed to see not Blanche's fear alone but all the fear in the world.

"My child," she said brokenly, "you cannot possibly harbor within yourself the fear of the whole universe—" She stopped.

There was a brief silence. Then Madame Lidoine said almost shyly: "You believe then that your fear—is religious?"

Blanche sighed deeply: "O Reverend Mother," she breathed, "consider the secret of my name!"

My friend, instead of discussing this most peculiar interview I shall quote the journal of Madame Lidoine. You have already seen that her notes which were for the most part purely factual could take the tone of religious revelation. Here they rise to the heights of mysticism. The very beginning of the paragraphs in question is clearly distinguished from all that went before. Instead of a date there is the heading: "The soul cries out to God." And the following is written in the form of a prayer:

O God, who art wisdom endless and profound and that cannot be gauged! Illumine Thy servant in the office Thou hast confided unto her. Thou knowest, O Lord, that I am ready to fulfill Thy commands instantly and as soon as Thou dost deign to communicate them to me. There is only danger that I may not fully understand them. Dear God, my reason I open to Thee like a book. Obliterate whatever is not pleasing to Thee and underline that which corresponds to Thy divine will. O Lord, can it be possible that Thou, who can increase the virtues of man beyond the bounds of nature, has also glorified a failing of the human soul in like wise? Is Thy mercy so great that Thou hast divined and understood the weakness of a poor soul who cannot overcome it, and that this very weakness Thou hast merged with Thy love?

These lines refer to Blanche beyond a doubt. For soon afterward she writes:

Was it Thy will, O Jesus, to choose the timid temperament of this poor child, so that while others are preparing to exult in the dying of Thy death, Thou hast communicated to her Thy mortal fear?

Was this the adoration that was still lacking to Thee and was I about to deprive Thee of it?

The next pages are concerned exclusively with this last question. But then we read:

> I have called upon Thee, O Lord, in complete submission of my will, my reason and all my strength, to make known to me Thy decision, so that I may clearly understand it. And so I do not believe that I can be mistaken. Thou art silent, dear God, and so Thou commandest me to keep silence also.

I think I am right in interpreting this last sentence as Madame Lidoine's decision to leave to God the question whether Blanche's fear was a part of her religious fervor. This reservation of judgment on her part would coincide with the practice of the Church in most cases of mysticism.

And so, for the time being, Blanche remained in Carmel of Compiègne. And under the direction of Madame Lidoine! For at this time she quite suddenly removed Sister Marie de l'Incarnation from the office of novice mistress and assumed its duties herself.

From this point on there is conflict between Marie de l'Incarnation and the Prioress.

It is of course out of the question that there was any conscious protest. The soul of this nun could not possibly have opposed her Prioress openly. She accepted her removal from office with exemplary poise. Neither did her personal humiliation alter her relations to the young novice. Sometimes she would say impulsively: "Oh, that timid little thing! I think she would run away from a mouse!" But she said these things without asperity and it is certain that she never stopped praying for Blanche. One can only speak of a conflict with Madame Lidoine if one recalls her viewpoint concerning the prohibition of final vows. For the time being it expressed itself only in a very justifiable concern about Blanche's sojourn in the convent. For now danger was really in the offing. But just as before the attitude of the former novice mistress communicated itself to the entire convent.

My friend, I do not intend to tabulate public events. You have guessed that the period I am discussing was that of the struggle for a lay code for the clergy, that is to say an oath of allegiance of the clergy to the government. And in the course of the Revolution this struggle degenerated into persecution of the Church. So the attitude of the convent of Compiègne to Blanche was quite understandable.

"We have no use for anybody now who will spoil our happiness", said even the mild Sister Jeanne de l'Enfance de Jésus. "Only think that next Christmas we may be celebrating in Heaven with *le petit Roi!*"

And the naïve little nun Constance de Saint Denis added with precocious wisdom, "And if it should really come to persecution, could we all say with a clear conscience that we will be strong enough to bear it?"

"No, my child, we certainly could not say that," said Madame Lidoine, who was just passing, in her deep voice, "but fortunately it is not necessary. For if such persecutions should really occur, His Majesty will have to have mercy on those who are strong among us as well as on those who are weak."

"But surely on the weak before all?" asked Constance de Saint Denis a little uncertainly when Madame Lidoine had gone. She expressed what they were all thinking and so no one answered but they looked at Blanche.

It is difficult to describe her as she was in those days. Madame Lidoine has left us no psychological revelations and whatever she had to say about the mystic nature of the case I have already quoted. Her notes contain only slight practical suggestions, such as this: "I have advised the poor child to continue seeking peace in fear itself, since God, as it seems, has no intention of freeing her from this emotion."

"Consolation in fear", "shelter in fear", "resignation in fear"—these are the recurring formulas of Madame Lidoine. She even advises Blanche to be "loyal to fear." I emphasize this last phrase, because, as far as I can see, it became decisive for Blanche. We learn that under the guidance of the Prioress she gave herself up to special veneration of the Eucharist, "of the unprotected God", as Madame Lidoine said. She uttered this on the occasion of the first blasphemies that were suddenly springing up in Catholic France in mockery of processions and other rites of the Christian religion.

Even to the spectator it seemed a curious coincidence that the same spring that saw the coming of stormy conflicts between the Church and the State in France, was also witness to the beatification of the great French Carmelite, Madame Acarie. (You recall, my friend, that it was at her grave that Marie de l'Incarnation had first felt her call to the convent.) Naturally Catholics in France and especially the Carmelite orders of the country interpreted this event as the last solemn challenge to save the religion of the nation. In Compiègne too, preparations for the celebration of the new saint were made in this spirit. But let us discard here at once all illusions of pontifical masses or illuminations which usually accompany a beatification. They considered themselves lucky in having a priest who had not as yet sworn the oath of allegiance to the government and who said a Mass honoring the saint. For the rest—they could not even purchase a worthy image of the new saint because all the Church money had been seized. However they found comfort in meditating upon the example the Carmelite nun had set her Sisters.

Chapter Seven

t was May, and on the altar of the chapel stood the image of the Mother of God with *le petit Roi* in her arms. His little head had been restored but the great scar at the neck was painfully visible and there was, of course, no crown! Old Jeanne de l'Enfance de Jésus had substituted a wreath of flowers. You can easily imagine that Marie de l'Incarnation was particularly concerned with the celebration of this saint and felt dissatisfied with these modest preparations.

On the eve of the festival a messenger appeared at the turn of the convent and delivered a note which contained there words: "Reverend Sisters, tomorrow intercede with your new saint for him whose threatened crown defends that of your little King." The note was written by Madame Elizabeth of France and had reference to the King's resistance to the civil code for the clergy. (You know, my friend, how much this contributed to the fall of the monarchy!) It is unnecessary to say that in Carmel de Compiègne Sister Marie de l'Incarnation was most deeply stirred by this incident. Let us realize the essentials once more: she believed that she had been called to a religious life at the grave of Madame Acarie, to do penance for the sins of the court to which she owed her existence. The words of Madame Elizabeth must have affected her simultaneously as a challenge to her royal blood and her own most personal mission in life. At this instant she resolved not merely to prepare herself and the convent under her sway for martyrdom, but to consecrate herself to this martyrdom.

"The kingdom of France which ignored its true mission so often, has lifted the banner of Christ", she said to Madame Lidoine. "Permit us, Reverend Mother, in this struggle for the rights of the Church to offer it whatever help God allows us to give. Permit us to heighten immeasurably the celebration in honor of our new saint by offering the Majesty of God our own lives for the preservation of His threatened Church in France."

Well, my dear friend, I no longer need to assure you that such acts of consecration were entirely in keeping with the principles of a Carmelite convent, and, do not let us deceive ourselves, we must recognize in this state of mind the last and strongest reserves of Christianity in the face of ultimate peril. (For what does the persecution of Christians mean if not this: that the sacrificial death of Christ, which was a voluntary act, is repeated by the members of His mystical body. In this sense then no Christian martyr ever has death forced upon him from without!)

And yet at that time Madame Lidoine hesitated to give her consent. But she did not do so because she wanted to withhold herself and her daughters from sacrifice. Remember her attitude concerning the prohibition of the final vows.

("What is Thy will with me?") She only felt that this sacrifice had not yet been willed by God. And she justified her refusal by pointing to the possibility of some who were weak in the community.

Marie de l'Incarnation had understood. There was only one weak soul in the convent of Carmel! "O Reverend Mother," she cried with sudden passion, and at such moments the veins in her temples swelled as the rivers of France swell in a storm, "O Reverend Mother, why do you bow the heroism of your daughters under the yoke of weakness of this one poor child? Her name is la Force but truly she should rather be called *la Faiblesse!*"

"Her name is Jésus au Jardin de l'Agonie", Madame Lidoine answered simply. Ah! it was the tragedy of this woman that even in her most divine moments she remained so quiet with her big daughter, so devoid of pathos!

The pale ascetic face of Marie de l'Incarnation was stricken with sorrow: one could almost hear the rivers of France rushing in her temples. "I understand", she said with ineffable nobility, "Reverend Mother, you do not wish God to have at His will the heroism of your daughters but—" The word "will" had given her sudden pause!

"Oh, yes! Why not heroism too?" Madame Lidoine returned her question. But her words seemed intolerably slow and heavy to Marie de l'Incarnation. At this moment it was really most unfortunate that either consciously or not she had always overlooked the Prioress.

Well, dear friend, I do not wish to pry among the shortcomings of a great spirit. Low-growing trees are rarely struck by lightning; small white clouds breed no storms; shallow waters do not tend to destroy whole tracts of land! To speak in the language of my heroines: the devil gives important testimony, for verily he seldom seeks out small souls. Who can marvel that he prefers to be housed in lofty shining dwellings? Let us be honest: the Revolution was such a dwelling! My dear, both you and I hailed this new dawning of humanity and how cruelly we were disappointed! For the tragedy is not that chaotic impulses lead to chaotic conditions, that wrong thinking unleashes passions and crimes! The real and terrible tragedy of humanity is that at a certain moment her loftiest ideals (such as liberty and fraternity!) become a caricature and are transformed into the direct opposite of themselves. Of course this does not mean that all our ideals were false, but it does mean, my friend, that they were inadequate.

And now a frightful plunge! Before the outbreak of any terror there is always a strange and solemn moment when all who are concerned are suddenly aware of the inexorable certainty of what is coming. Do you remember those breathless August days before the downfall of the monarchy? (Ah, my friend, even a weak king is an incomparable bulwark of strength: not in the branches of a tree do force and power reside, but in its roots!) Whence came the sudden specter of Satan? This uncanny crawling approach of the dark, the inarticulate? Who summoned it? Who told us that it was inevitable? Who forced our humane concepts, so confident of victory, to capitulate? Did it not seem as if every leaf on the trees of France trembled with us? All trembled! Those who craved horror and those who resisted it desperately!

This horror was the last dreadful union of all. But it is impossible to describe those hours! One can understand them only if one has lived through them, if one has shuddered through every frightful moment.

At that time Monsignore Rigaud informed the Prioress Lidoine de Saint Augustin that he wished to speak to her. Do not be amazed at this journey, my friend. The full rigor of seclusion had abated in those days. Soon it was to be abolished entirely. Members of orders realized clearly that they were to be driven forth from their convents and monasteries. Even religious dress, that final, most intimate symbol of seclusion from the world, had already been abandoned. In response to the demand of the government, the orders, devoid of all means of their own, had bidden their members to apply to their families for lay clothing.

So Madame Lidoine hastened to Paris to receive the last commands of her superior for the difficult times that were at hand. She left Sister Marie de l'Incarnation to take her place during her absence. You may be surprised at this arrangement. I believe it was intended as a mark of confidence in her resisting Sister and also perhaps in the strength of her office.

And so the course of events seems all the more tragic.

We were just speaking of the inevitable certainty of all. But there was one person in Paris who was excluded from it. It was Madame de Chalais who came to Compiègne to bring Blanche the lay clothing she had requested of her father.

Madame de Chalais had changed very little. The solidness of her character and of her convictions had survived these troubled times as effectively as her too tight bodice triumphed over the new style of flexible waistline. It was infinitely consoling to hear how steadfastly she held to the idea that the exemplary piety of such a good king as France boasted of, could not possibly remain unrewarded. That if it really came to the utmost, the good Christian nobles and the Swiss who were gathered in the Tuileries would undoubtedly conquer the wild and heathen people and that Destiny simply would not allow the threatening of really worthy priests.

I assume that Madame de Chalais expressed herself something like this at Compiègne. Her interview with Blanche is not recorded but I do not think it was particularly important. It is enough to say that Madame de Chalais saw her pupil after a considerable lapse of time and, since lay clothing was worn, she saw her unveiled. I have already stated that it is somewhat difficult to describe Blanche but she must have had something very clearly defined about her, above all something utterly different from what Madame de Chalais had expected. I am almost tempted to believe that she enacted a scene with Blanche that was like the one that had taken place once upon a time at the banister of the stairs. At any rate, Madame de Chalais returned from the reception room in high excitement.

"Is it really true that you believe that one can no longer depend upon God?" she asked of the Sister who had charge of the turn. She was in great perturbation. "Do you really believe that in a Carmelite convent? What a disgrace!" After these words she felt faint. They wished to call Blanche but she prevented them from doing this in great terror. So they gave her a chair and held smelling salts to her nose and gradually she recovered. But she burst into tears. No one could remember ever having seen her cry!

"O God," she sobbed, "O God, they will storm the Tuileries and drive away the King! They will depose him!" (Observe that she said "they will", and not "intend to"!) "They will kill him, the best and most God-fearing of all kings!" (Most God-fearing!) "They will slaughter the faithful priests" (faithful!), "they will murder the good Swiss" (good!). "Everything is wild chaos and we are making straight for the most terrible anarchy and the best, of course, will perish!" (Best!)

So she wailed to the poor nuns and in doing so mercilessly disclosed to them the desperate state of affairs in France. Obviously Madame Lidoine had kept the worst from them.

In order to quiet her they showed her a picture of *le petit Roi* but she hardly glanced at it. "Ah!" she cried, "*le petit Roi* is dead!" But she did not add as Blanche had done one Christmas night: "Now there is only the living Christ!" It seemed as if all her faith were suddenly at an end. Even her outward appearance was altered and dreadful. Her tight bodice was open. The whalebones had cracked when she sank into the proffered seat and jutted pitifully through the crushed silk of her dress. Her proud coiffure resembled a nest in which a cat has prowled. From time to time she fingered her gaunt neck as if to convince herself that it was still safe between her shoulders. Then she expressed her desire to travel to Switzerland, to Germany, Spain or Belgium. In short, in her imagination she fled across all the borders of her country only to return again to her own despair. But we cannot dwell further on the distress of this poor old woman. Suffice to say that they finally persuaded her to enter her carriage by telling her that if she really wanted to flee there was no time to be lost. (I heard later that she reached the border successfully but died in Brussels three days later.)

And now of Carmel de Compiègne! Imagine, my friend, on what ground Madame de Chalais' words fell! Remember that Sister Marie de l'Incarnation was taking the place of the Prioress! Without a doubt her office gave her the opportunity of initiating a step which Madame Lidoine had rejected, it is true, but not actually forbidden. (We shall never find Marie de l'Incarnation on the road of positive disobedience but always on narrow bypaths.) You have guessed which step I mean: it was a question of the last possible priceless moment for the heroic consecration to the salvation of France.

It appears that some of the Carmelite nuns were dismayed at Marie de l'Incarnation's proposal. For indeed it was no longer a matter of "stringing colored glass beads", to quote Madame Lidoine's words, for at that time the guillotine had already been established on the Grève Square. Nevertheless the convent consented bravely, though the Sisters grew more or less pale. Only little naïve Constance de Saint Denis confessed, half crying, that she would be very much afraid if she had to be the last to mount the scaffold.

This confession was very painful to Marie de l'Incarnation: "But you know that among the members of the order the youngest never goes last but the eldest, and besides you are not even the youngest but—" Not until this moment did she look at Blanche whom she had forgotten in her perturbation. "At this moment", Madame Lidoine writes later, "the shadow of Christ's mortal fear embarked on its voyage of heroism, but she did not recognize it!" This is an excuse for the erring of this noble soul but it is also a heavy accusation!

And yet Sister Marie de l'Incarnation felt something of that shadow. When she looked at Blanche she felt a strange oppression something like that of Madame de Chalais. But it was not the fear of sacrifice, it was rather the fear of hindrance to her own sacrifice. And now we reach the point when she knew: we cannot wait any longer, and also: we must be certain of our strength. For they were well aware that at some time or other they would be called upon to realize in action the words of the consecration.

"I am compelling no one to make this promise", she said quickly. "Whoever cannot overcome herself enough to offer Christ her life of her own free will, whoever does not feel this inexpressible ecstasy, let her remain aside." Undoubtedly she thought that Blanche would avail herself of this permission, and, let us be honest, she even wished it! For in this case, remaining aside meant excluding herself from the community, and so symbolized the first step to removal. But Blanche did not exclude herself and did not remain aside.

Let us briefly visualize the procedure of such acts of

consecration. Personal vows are usually made silently during Mass immediately after transubstantiation. It is customary to inform the officiating priest. He refers to the vow in his memento and later gives communion and his blessing.

Chapter Eight

To continue again from the journal of Madame Lidoine. After her return from the city, this faithful and motherly woman did everything within her power to fathom the poor child's state of mind during and after the vow. The night before was spent in silent preparation. Now, my friend, we should greatly underestimate Marie de l'Incarnation's power over the human soul if we doubted that on the next morning all were in excellent condition. All, of course, except Blanche! Before going to Mass Marie de l'Incarnation made one more attempt to detain her. The emotions of the young novice can be inferred from her words on this occasion:

"My child," she said to her, "if you could only realize that no one is demanding this vow from you! Do you really wish to appear before the Saviour with this mortal fear in your heart?"

And Blanche replied: "Reverend Mother, I do not wish to be disloyal." (Let us remember, my friend, the formula that Madame Lidoine had underscored in her journal: "to remain loyal to fear.")

We know that Blanche entered the chapel with the others. Little Constance de Saint Denis who was walking beside her, recalls it distinctly. "But," she said, "I did not dare to look at her face, for on that morning we were all seized by a great oppressive happiness which made us very vulnerable."

And now the consecration itself! My dear friend, I still see before me a little chapel which the hand of the State had despoiled of all adornment, the altars empty as on Good Friday. I see a choir without chairs. In Carmelite convents there are no comforts. I see women kneeling on the wooden floors, women who are praying at a silent Mass accompanied from afar by the *Ça ira* in the streets. The faces of these women are strangely luminous. They are filled with the bliss of complete surrender, of unreserved and overwhelming willingness that has already passed beyond the pale of life and death. But I am like Constance de Saint Denis. Ah! my dear, there is one of these women I dare not visualize. I cannot endure the sight of a face small and pinched, wet with perspiration, distorted by terror—or rather by the terror of all France, of Eternal Love itself! Constance de Saint Denis relates that during the transubstantiation, that is to say, while they were making the vow, Blanche was still kneeling beside her. But when they rose to take communion she was missing! (Ah! hers was to be a very different communion!)

Well, my friend, none will gainsay us if we state that at the time Blanche's nerves failed her. But we could state the matter in quite another way too! "Poor child," writes Madame Lidoine de Saint Augustin, "it was she who wanted to share

76

the mortal fear of the Saviour and when her strength broke, she ran into the very heart of fear itself!"

I pass over Blanche's flight, for unfortunately it is not only a question of leaving the chapel, but of quitting the convent. A few days later the Prioress received a letter from the Marquis de la Force in which he informed her that his daughter had reached Paris in a deplorable condition and was now ill. I cannot resist quoting at least a few sentences from the Marquis' letter. For Monsieur de la Force had suffered a change of heart no less astonishing in its way than that of Madame de Chalais! He had discovered that certain ideas were not content with furbishing his conversation with witty phrases, but had an odd tendency to demand realization with complete disregard as to the means to this end. As a result the Marquis was now all for a strong monarchy and absolute authority. He even surprised himself and his entourage by recognizing the need for religion and above all for the Church. The very first procession of the negators of God had shocked him profoundly. (Heavens! It is true that atheism is cruder stuff in the coarse hands of the mob than on the subtle lips of aristocrats!)

"This outrage is intolerable!" he is said to have declared at the time. "Something ought to be done about it! Religious people should see to it. I am told that they still exist in sufficient numbers. I hope they will increase. These circles are indispensable for the maintenance of law and order. Why don't they do something? Do the convents and monasteries believe that prayer and sacrifice will overcome these dangerous outbreaks? That would be a fatal error!" So Monsieur de la Force wrote to everyone including Madame Lidoine. But I am only mentioning this in elucidation of what followed. For unfortunately we can no longer ascertain whether the poor Marquis intended this time to face the results of his theories. For Life took the initiative and faced them in his stead, and as far as I can see, the actual events were the logical consequences of the beliefs that he had held up to this point: early in September Monsieur de la Force together with many of his friends who were ardent advocates of freedom, found himself in prison!

Chapter Nine

nd now, my friend, I shall continue my story from a different angle, for from this point on I myself was a spectator of what I have to tell you. You know that in those days there was a rumor in our Paris circles to the effect that you too were among the imprisoned aristocrats. So, disguised as one of my servants, I hastened from one prison to another. I even wore the tricolor! But spare me a description of my state of mind! In the meantime your carriage was already approaching the safe shores of the Rhine. My friend, how I should like to refrain from reminding you of these things! But here it is not a question of conjuring up fear and terror or of satisfying perverse curiosity. Still, I cannot avoid doing these very things because it is my duty. My friend, fear is a great emotion. Not one of us was sufficiently afraid! Society should be afraid. A State should know fear. Governments should tremble. To tremble is to be strong. These things I am writing of have taken place and may reoccur at any moment!

It was pure coincidence that I happened to enter a prison

courtyard at the very moment they were killing the Marquis de la Force. It was at night. The courtyard was filled with people. Did I say people, human beings? Never before had such creatures been seen in Paris! Where had they come from? What dreadful change had converted the populace into this bloodthirsty rabble? (Ah! my friend, this very change—that is just what we are concerned with!) There was a pervasive reek of wine. Everyone was horribly drunk and filled with brutal and ghastly gaiety. Pikes leaned against the inner gates of the prison like a forest of stark trees. Torches burned at either side of the entrance and lit up this forest with a red, menacing glare. From time to time the gates opened and admitted one or more human forms. A sound of pikes, a few screams and all was over. (You know that this continued for several days and nights.)

I staggered from corpse to corpse to convince myself that you were not among the victims. The mob that followed the bloody spectacle desecrated some of these bodies most horribly. Again the gate of terror opened: the crowd was silent as a lowering animal. Suddenly I felt that no individual person was present at all. I could distinguish no one but the victims. Every time I tried to see one person alone, he merged with everyone else. Involuntarily I leaned against the wall to await the cry of agony of the only other person there besides myself. But I heard nothing. There was only a wild chaos of voices—then it stopped and there was breathless silence.

All at once I heard the short clear cry of a girl: "*Vive la nation!*" It was not loud but it penetrated to the marrow of one's bones. It was not a cry of fear but rather of love. I had never heard anything like it. Not terrible, but utterly strange, almost transcending. This cry sounded as if a soul had been released from matter and knew nothing more of the limitations of the flesh. I could not help opening my eyes.

The courtyard was filled with indescribable tumult. They were crowding about someone I could not see. *"Vive la nation! Vive la nation!"* the mob bellowed with fanatic joy. Then I saw how a very old man and a young girl were lifted on ready shoulders: they were Mademoiselle de Sombreuil and her father.

Well, my dear friend, you know the tale of this famous martyr to filial devotion, for the name of Sombreuil is included in your list of the heroines of the Revolution. Somebody called out to me that this girl had just emptied a cup of the blood of dead aristocrats to the health of the nation! This was the price these inhuman scoundrels had demanded for the life of her father! In the meantime the gruesome procession approached. And it was a triumphal procession too! The two who had only just been threatened with death had become the heralded heroes of the people. They were carried by quite close to me. They say that Mademoiselle de Sombreuil had been a fair and blooming girl. I do not know if this was so. The person I saw seemed wholly bodiless to me. You will not believe me, but she looked ecstatic, as if she knew nothing of fear or disgust but only that her father had been saved.

The procession disappeared through the outer gate. The

mob followed. An empty alley formed toward the prison: on the ground I saw the body of Monsieur de la Force and behind him, leaning against the wall, his daughter Blanche. A nasty little fellow in a red cap stood in front of her. Of course he was not the same one who had entered her cell, and yet through some infernal intuition he seemed to know who she was. Or did her rigidly folded hands betray the nun? Or her short hair? The fellow was holding a cup in his hand and made a blasphemous gesture. (My friend, you know of these things for you have seen the negators of God going about.) "Take communion, Citizeness", he screamed, and put the cup forcibly to her lips. Obviously it was the one Mademoiselle de Sombreuil had just emptied to save her father's life. Ah! my friend, she at least had had the significance of sacrifice to uphold her. Here there was only meaningless brutality. Or was there a meaning after all? Did this girl at that moment embody her martyred country which was being forced to drink the blood of its children? Horror of horrors! I closed my eyes again.

But already the mob shrieked its crazy *"Vive la nation! Vive la nation."* It was over.

Some women near me grumbled, "But why don't they lift up this fine young woman too! Is she supposed to walk through the dirt?" (By "dirt" they meant the spilled blood covering the ground!)

They lifted Blanche to their shoulders and carried her past me in triumph. How shall I describe her to you? I must confess that I did not recognize her at all! Her face was completely devoid of expression, not bodiless spirit like that of

82

Mademoiselle de Sombreuil, but shrunk entirely into itself
—gone! Her short hair that hung about her face in frightful
disorder seemed to me a symbol of the dissolution of her
personality. (My friend, there is still another death than the
one Marie de l'Incarnation had in mind.)

The crowd continued to bellow *"Vive la nation"* without respite. A band of musicians joined in, the *Carmagnole*
started up, everyone began to move. I felt that it would be
dangerous to remain in the empty courtyard and joined the
procession. A few women marched next to me. They were
the same who had called out before that it was a shame to let
Blanche walk through the dirt. They assured me that they
would accompany her to the residence of the de la Force
family and see to it that the little citizeness got her supper
all right. And I am sure that they really attempted to do this!
Ah! my friend, do not think that these people were not capable of good impulses. The mob is always capable of good
impulses! That is the very thing that makes a mob of people:
that they are capable of anything at all!

As for me, I was convinced at the time that Blanche would
not live through the night. This thought was a solace to me.
But Blanche did continue to live—or rather to exist. If in
that dreadful September night she had been the symbol of
our unhappy country, there was in this continuance of suffering a sort of tragic rightness. How it was possible, I mean
from Blanche's point of view, I did not know and in a deeper
sense it is almost irrelevant. I might imagine that she herself knew nothing of her own existence any more. What
actually happened to her is this: we have witnesses to the

fact that she maintained her position of a favorite with the mob, that this most moody and changeable of all rulers continued to be proud of her deed. Ah! nothing bears greater testimony to the ruin of her personality than the terrible consideration accorded to her. If we are to believe a legend that circulated in Paris, the women were careful to minister to the needs of their young heroine. We know that some of them established themselves in the home of the murdered Marquis. They were seen there, their broad bodies squeezed between the gilded arms of the sofas, their knitting in their hands, the remnants of their meals strewn over the parquet floors. These meals they shared with Blanche. Then in the evening their husbands and lovers appeared. Such at least is my conjecture. The bloody events of the day were discussed. They sang the *Carmagnole*. They danced! Perhaps they even danced with Blanche. I seem to see her little hopeless figure going through the steps, as distinctly as I remember her on the shoulders of the mob on that September night. But let me say once more that fundamentally these details are not important, and that I cannot be positive about them either. Some say, and I consider this more probable, that in those days Blanche crouched in the corner of a rear room alone and in complete apathy; that only occasionally she was dragged out to participate in some mass procession of women or in some political parade through the streets of Paris. "We had to do that from time to time", I was told later by one of her dreadful September mothers who in the interval had become an honest market vendor again. "For the poor lady was an aristocrat by birth and besides she had been a nun and there were such fanatic people in the government. You probably remember, Monsieur."

Oh, yes, I remember! So it was merely a protective measure! My friend, nothing can exceed the loyalty of one of these September women!

And how this question occurs to us: Were these atrocities known in the Carmelite convent of Compiègne? I think it is fairly certain that this is not the case, but that the letter written by the Marquis de la Force was the last news they had of Blanche. (This is not surprising, my friend, for we are now launched upon the sea of chaos!) In Madame Lidoine's journal of this period there is no mention of the former novice. But neither is there any mention of the consecration of Marie de l'Incarnation and of Marie de l'Incarnation herself who had figured so largely before! This silence is most eloquent. It is broken only on the day on which the King was executed. Beyond a doubt the convent was deeply shocked at this event and interpreted it as a rejection of their will to sacrifice. Let us not forget that Marie de l'Incarnation's dedication took place on the eve of the storming of the Tuileries—that for this woman of royal blood the salvation of religious France had always been bound up with the security of the crown! Madame Lidoine informs us that at that time she comforted her weeping Sisters with the words: "*Le roi est mort, vive le roi!*" By implication this referred to the unhappy little dauphin, for Madame Lidoine continues her journal with her own thoughts on this subject: "And so, O God, Thou hast permitted the king of our home on earth to become a small weak child like *le petit Roi de Gloire!*"

And then with clear recognition of inevitable chaos: "It is then Thy divine will that we bring Thee a sacrifice without hope, unless that Thy ways be inscrutable!"

Chapter Ten

nd now, my friend, we come to the preparation for the second act of consecration in the Carmelite convent in Compiègne. This time Madame Lidoine is the initiator. It is the preparation of inevitable sacrifice or, in her own words, "the sacrifice that is predestined"; but at the same time it is the preparation for unconditioned sacrifice. "Sacrifice without hope, sacrifice for God alone, sacrifice without heroism, sacrifice only through God, sacrifice in the dark of the night, a sacrifice in the midst of chaos"—these are the phrases that occur continually in her journal. She does not say "sacrifice to avert chaos"—this was no longer possible but what she had in mind is "sacrifice of absolute obedience" and "sacrifice of pure love." (My friend, I do not believe that she thought she was giving a new and increased value to sacrifice. This humble soul thought only of the special claims of her times.) Undoubtedly she was training the convent in this sense to expect a calamity. But what was the attitude of Marie de l'Incarnation to this altered meaning of sacrifice? I think it was already defined in the words, "*Vive le roi!*" Ah, my friend, in this slight remark the magnetic personality of that great Carmelite nun is revealed fully to us again! She was unbroken, unresigned! Obviously Blanche's flight to her father had relieved her immensely. I can almost hear her ask Madame Lidoine, "Reverend Mother, is it not a good thing that there is among us no longer anyone who might falter?" (The Prioress quotes this remark frequently. Apparently Marie de l'Incarnation repeated it often.) If we were trying to establish the presence of a sense of guilt in her, we might detect it in this oft-repeated phrase. But we can determine no guilt—at least no conscious guilt! This is probably the reason for Madame Lidoine's silence concerning the first act of consecration. She did not wish to anticipate an hour that had not yet been willed by God. But that hour had already come!

At this time the Carmelite nuns of the Rue d'Enfer found means to inquire of the convent of Compiègne if there was any possibility of sending *le petit Roi de Gloire*—or the sad remains of that little figure—secretly to Paris so that He might be closer to the little Prince, or "save him", as Marie de l'Incarnation said. (Ah! she did not realize what it signified that the dauphin was in the hands of the shoemaker Simon!) She herself had been called to Paris at that time by the authorities on the question of her income. (You recall, my friend, that this was her inheritance from the court.) Madame Lidoine writes that she hailed these dangerous summons with rejoicing because she thought she would have the opportunity of testifying to her love for Christ. Of course she consented at once, without any scruples or fears, to arrange for the transfer of *le petit Roi de Gloire* on this occasion.

The ancient Sister Jeanne de l'Enfance de Jésus wept at parting for she had been caring for *le petit Roi* for almost eighty years. On the very last day He was in the convent she had sewed Him a little coat for the journey (made of an old mended habit). Of course it was crooked again just as the shirt had been at Christmas. Still in the inventory of His wardrobe that was sent along with *le petit Roi*, it figured as "the mantle of the crown", just as in the past when it had been of purple cloth embroidered with gold.

Now, my dear friend, I must say that I consider it absurd to give credence to the rumor that this touching little inventory of His wardrobe which was later seized in the Rue de l'Enfer (*le petit Roi* Himself fell into the hands of His foes at that time) was the cause of the misfortune of Carmel de Compiègne. It is true that the accusation read: the nuns had attempted to hide the mantle of the crown and that the three poor little shirts all cut awry which accompanied *le petit Roi* had been destined for little Capet! But you know that such absurdities were daily occurrences. My friend, this mantle of the crown was only the cloak for an unpardonable undertaking. And in this accusation the name of Capet was used in lieu of that of *le petit Roi* Himself. The whole affair had already been decided upon when Marie de l'Incarnation was summoned to Paris.

The lawyer Sézille, who was her counsel during the proceedings, believed from the first that this business of her income was only a pretext to seize her person, since she was considered the most important member of her order; that this suit against her was simply the preface to other proceedings with which priests who had not sworn the oath of allegiance to the government and the members of dissolved orders were persecuted. (You know that the people had decided to reverence Reason alone! Ah! but Reason was betrayed as well as Faith!)

Lawyer Sézille feared for his client at the very outset. Perhaps he was also afraid of the passionate fervor she would reveal to the tribunal. At least I think this was the reason why he asked Madame Lidoine to come to Paris also. In spite of his misgivings, however, matters went off smoothly. Marie de l'Incarnation was too wise to give her enemies the triumph of appearing to have accused her with any semblance of right. She desired real martyrdom!

Monsieur Sézille admits that she faced her accusers with incredible dignity and consummate wisdom. And indeed she was quite calm. And this must have been the reason why the heart-rending news of the fate of the dauphin which she received in Paris, did not discourage her. (The Carmelites in the Rue de l'Enfer were only bent upon bringing *le petit Roi* to sick children so that He might help them to die!) It was certain that the Carmelites would be brought to court. Questions that were put, the manner in which the affair was drawn out and extended to other fields, revealed that there were ulterior motives involved.

Monsieur Sézille expressed this idea clearly, when, after the affair of Marie de l'Incarnation's income had been arranged, he accompanied the Carmelites to the stage coach.

They were in the Rue des Prêtres de Saint Paul, where it intersects with the Rue Saint Antoine. At this moment it was crowded with excited people. In the midst of the gathering the lawyer observed one of those carts in which the unfortunate victims of the guillotine were brought to the Place de la Revolution. In order to spare his clients the sorry sight, Monsieur Sézille cast about for an excuse to enter a nearby house, but the burning eyes of Marie de l'Incarnation had already seen! "No, Monsieur Sézille," she said quickly, "I see priests on that cart. Suffer us to gather strength by admiring the servants of Christ on their way to the place of execution! For you just implied yourself that we must hold ourselves in readiness to go that way also." Then turning to Madame Lidoine she added, "Is it not fortunate, Reverend Mother, that there is no one among us who is not ready to —" As she spoke, and it was the last time she defended her act of consecration, she suddenly grew pale and broke off in the middle of her sentence.

Madame Lidoine and the lawyer followed the direction of her gaze; it passed beyond the unhappy victims on the cart and fixed itself rigidly upon a group of women who had joined the procession. My friend, you know about those women who accompanied the carts to the guillotine, so I shall omit any comments.

"Christ in Heaven, now do I understand Thy mortal fear", she cried, and immediately followed the procession and disappeared in the crowd. Madame Lidoine and the lawyer looked at each other in amazement. They waited a few minutes but Marie de l'Incarnation did not return. In the meantime the stage coach was ready to leave for Compiègne and Madame Lidoine had to make up her mind to go alone. Upon her return she was arrested together with the whole convent.

In the evening Marie de l'Incarnation reached the house of her lawyer in a condition of complete exhaustion. He was a dry and sober man—good heavens, he had to be for he was an excellent lawyer—but even he noticed at once that some great change or conflict had taken place within her. "She resembled a ship", he told me later, "whose masts move as in a storm although the air is quiet." Still she was able to tell him with outer calm that on that morning she had recognized a former novice of the convent among the women who were accompanying the cart, and that she had hastened after her to release her from her frightful companions. But her attempt had been in vain. The girl she was looking for had disappeared as if the earth had swallowed her up. I understand this: my friend, do you recall my feelings on that September night when I yielded to the gruesome illusion that there were no longer any individuals? Ah! chaos is a terrible parody on the equality of all! In chaos none preserves even his own face. The small expressionless features of Blanche could no longer be distinguished from all the rest. It is remarkable that Marie de l'Incarnation had recognized them at all! Even if only for an instant! Now she herself assumed that she had been mistaken and seemed to find consolation in that thought. Nevertheless she asked her lawyer to make inquiries as to the whereabouts of the former novice, while she herself followed the Prioress back to the convent, a course of action which obedience, so she said, prescribed. But in the meantime it had become impossible to leave Paris. All the gates were under guard for several days, a regulation not uncommon in those times. Marie de l'Incarnation could not leave the city. And soon the news of the arrest of the Carmelite nuns of Compiègne arrived! Marie de l'Incarnation, who had been the very soul of sacrifice, was the only one who had escaped, who had been excluded from the sacrifice!

Chapter Eleven

t that time I had my first interview with her. Monsieur Sézille, who had come to me in the course of his searches for Blanche, took me to her. I did not suspect how much my memories of those September days must mean to her. She received me with the request to speak openly without trying to spare her. And this I did. My friend, I told her about Blanche's dreadful fate. She listened to me with marvelous composure but suddenly I saw that she had lost all control of herself. It seemed as if she were emptying the same cup of horror that had been put to Blanche's lips. When I related the incident to her she trembled from head to foot. It was a most peculiar experience to see this great and noble woman, whose every feature was marked with fearlessness, tremble so violently. I assure you, my friend, that never, not even on that September night, did I behold on the faces of the murdered victims so complete an expression of horror as on the most heroic lineaments I ever saw! It would have been insulting to offer her a word of consolation. I simply stated my conviction that Blanche could not possibly be alive.

She shook her head mournfully. (I felt that she had forgotten my presence entirely.) It was evident that at this moment she abandoned all hope.

"Oh, yes, she is alive", she said softly. "She is alive." And, with wonderful intuition, "Is not this poor country alive too? Is not the unhappy little King of France alive in all his agony?" And then as if she were plunging desperately into the depths of her own despair: "It is harder to live than to die! Life is more difficult than death!"

And now, my friend, comes the real sacrifice of this great soul. We see Marie de l'Incarnation approaching it and disappearing as through a dark gate—disappearing entirely. This sacrifice has no proud name. No one admired her for it, noted it down or even observed it! (For the only priest who knew of it in confessional will take his secret to the grave with him.) Madame Lidoine's journal ends with the day of her arrest, as may be expected. But Marie de l'Incarnation's biography of the Sisters keeps utter silence concerning herself. And yet hers is also a sacrifice of life itself for she silently effaced the significance of her whole life. And this significance was sacrifice itself!

Monsieur Sézille feared that she would try to rejoin the Sisters. This would have been easy as there was a warrant for her in whom the revolutionists hated both the soul of the convent and her royal blood. (As far as men were concerned, martyrdom should have been meted out to her before all.) But we know as a fact that during the entire proceedings she did not take the slightest step that might have endangered her, and submitted with admirable docility to all the precautions imposed upon her by the lawyer at whose house she was staying for the time being. He even confesses that her caution was so painfully conscientious that petty souls might have suspected that she was trembling for her life as the aristocrats were trembling for theirs. She knew perfectly well what was being said about her but she never made an attempt to justify herself.

The little singer Rose Ducor indeed, into whose house she moved in the course of events (she suffered this precautionary measure too without resistance), insisted from the very outset that this care on her part was exceptionally saintly. (You recall that it was Rose Ducor who later spread the legend of the stigmata on the neck of her guest.) For Rose believed that the Abbé Kiener, an old Alsatian priest who also was hiding in her house, had impressed Marie de l'Incarnation with the duty of preserving her life. "Marie de l'Incarnation", so Rose Ducor said, "submitted to life as if it were a heavy penance." (Ah! Rose Ducor did not dream to what extent she was speaking the truth!)

To support her opinion she tells of that last greeting which Marie de l'Incarnation tried to send to Madame Lidoine. It was a narrow strip of paper on which were only these words: "Give me the crown of martyrdom or withhold it from me."

The resolute little singer who counted her admirers in all circles hoped to win over a prison official to transmit the message hidden in a ring. But she could not do it. (My friend, such plans only succeed in fiction. Real life is far more merciless.) And so in this direction also the sacrifice of Marie de l'Incarnation ends in profound silence.

In the meantime the Carmelites of Compiègne had been conducted to the Conciergerie in Paris. Their suit was approaching its end. I described the details in a former letter. The whole thing was just as brief as it was typical. In such cases the outcome was fixed in the beginning. I do not hesitate to designate such predetermined judgments as the darkest pages in the history of the Revolution. (But perhaps chaos cannot be termed history. It was something beyond all history.)

On the feast day of Our Lady of Mount Carmel, these sixteen Carmelite nuns of Compiègne were condemned to death by the guillotine. Marie de l'Incarnation was included in this sentence. Try to imagine, my friend, what a storm of emotion this must have unleashed in her soul! Sézille informed her of the facts. He had done his honorable and hopeless duty in defending the sixteen Carmelite nuns.

Marie de l'Incarnation believed that her Sisters would mount the scaffold singing, for this had been prearranged in the convent. She begged the Abbé Kiener to be permitted to accompany him, for he had offered to give absolution to the condemned on the way to the place of execution. (Absolution disguised by the strains of the *Carmagnole* in the midst of the hooting crowd! That was the only possibility in those days!) But he refused her. "And this", Rose Ducor said later, "was a moment of most bitter sorrow to her."

"My father," she cried, bursting into tears, "you are robbing me of my last hope."

"And what is your hope?" he asked almost with severity.

At this question the full beautiful force of her personality broke through. She did not rebel. She was simply overwhelmed. "I wanted to sing too", she cried. "Oh, if I could only be the last, the very last for whom it is hardest of all!"

He answered, "Sacrifice your voice also, my daughter, yield up your voice to the very last one."

She wept again. "My father," she said, "my sacrifices have not been accepted. You know it. I shall be the most abandoned of all."

"Remember how Christ was abandoned," he answered gently, "and remember the silence of Mary."

Her resistance broke. "At that time", Rose Ducor reported later, "her face first showed that peculiar expression in which one could suddenly see how she must have looked as a child. It was as if an early, most lovely and delicate painting became visible under some splendid Baroque restoration." Without a word she crossed her arms on her breast.

And now, my friend, we have arrived at the question in your letter, the query concerning the touching voice of young Blanche de la Force.

Monsieur Sézille begged me to be present at the Place de la Revolution on that day. He wanted me to identify Blanche with the former novice, for he had learned that the women were going to bring her to the scaffold to witness the execution of the Carmelite nuns of Compiègne. (Another protective measure, most likely.) But do not think, my friend, that at this point I expect you to visualize the bloody guillotine! I myself cannot endure the sight of that horrible machine. Believe me, I had rather see a living executioner at work, a man who has the courage to wield the knife, and a hand of flesh and blood that knows at least that it is perpetrating an awful deed. Life should not be shattered by machinery. And yet this is the very symbol of our destiny. Ah! my friend, a machine cannot discriminate, it is not responsible, it shudders at nothing, it destroys indifferently everything that is brought to it, the noble and the pure as well as the most criminal. Truly, the machine is a worthy tool of chaos. Perhaps it is the very crown of chaos, a crown worn by the enthusiasm of the soulless mob that knows no divine creation but only satanic destruction.

I stood in the midst of the jeering crowd. Never have I felt the hopelessness of our position as desperately as then. You know that I am not tall. Chaos surged above me. I was lost in it. I actually could not see what happened. I could only hear. All my powers of perception centered in the sense of hearing and increased it incredibly.

The Carmelites arrived singing at the Place de la Revolution, just as Marie de l'Incarnation had expected. Their psalms could be heard from afar and penetrated the screams of the populace with strange clarity, or did the howls of the cruel audience cease at the sight of the victims? I could clearly distinguish the last words of the *Salve Regina* (this, you know, is sung at the deathbed of a nun) and soon afterward the first line of the *Veni Creator*. There was something light and lovely in their singing, something tender and yet strong and calm. Never would I have thought that such a song could leave the lips of those condemned to death. I had been deeply disturbed. But when I heard this singing I grew quiet. *Creator spiritus, Creator spiritus*, I seemed to hear these two words again and again. They seemed to cast anchor within me.

And the song flowed on full and clear. To judge by the sound, the cart must have been moving very slowly. Probably the crowd blocked the way. I had the feeling that they were still far from the square. For this singing effaced all sense of time, it effaced *space* and the bloody Place de la Revolution. It effaced the guillotine and *Creator spiritus, Creator spiritus!* It effaced even chaos. All at once I had the sensation of being among human creatures again. And at the same moment someone seemed to whisper into my ear: "France is not only drinking the blood of its children, it is spilling blood for them too, its purest and noblest blood." I started. There was absolute silence on the Place de la Revolution. (My friend, even at the execution of the King there had not been such utter stillness.) The song seemed lower too. Probably the cart had gone on, perhaps it had already reached its goal. My heart began to beat. And I became aware that a very high voice was lacking in the chorus—a moment later another. I had thought that the execution had not even begun and in reality it was almost over.

Now only two voices sustained the song. For a moment they floated like a shining rainbow over the Place de la Revolution. Then the one side was extinguished. Only the other continued to glow. But already the faded shimmer of the first was taken up by a second, a thin frail childish voice. I had the illusion that it was not coming from the heights of the scaffold but from the thick of the crowd, somewhere—just as if the crowd were making a response. (Lovely illusion!)

At the same moment the crowded lines were swayed by a violent upheaval. Right in front of me (just as on that September night) I saw an empty gap: I saw, and I saw exactly as on that night, Blanche de la Force in the seething mass of those dreadful women. Her small pinched face stood out from its surroundings and discarded those surroundings like a wrap or a shawl. I recognized the face in every feature and yet I did not recognize it. It was quite without fear! She was singing! With her small, weak, childish voice she sang without a tremor, exultingly as a bird! All alone across the great terrible square she sang the *Veni Creator* of her Sisters to the very end.

> Deo patri sit gloria
> Et filio, qui a mortuis
> Surrexit ac Paraclito
> In saeculorum saecula.

Distinctly I heard the profession of faith to the Trinity. The amen I did not hear. (You know that those furious women fell upon Blanche at once.) And now, my friend, the rainbow over the Place de la Revolution had died away. And yet I had the feeling that the Revolution was over. (As a matter of fact the Reign of Terror collapsed ten days later.)

When I entered the singer's house in company with the Alsatian Abbé a little girl I did not know was sitting on the steps. She came up to us confidingly and produced a small bundle she was carrying under her apron. She handed it to the priest: it was *le petit Roi de Gloire!* The child had found Him in the street covered with mud. Someone in some blasphemous procession must have thrown the little figure away.

Together we went to Marie de l'Incarnation. She looked like a Mater Dolorosa. The priest took her hand. "Come, Marie of the Incarnation", he said. In his native language the significance of her name became more evident. Or was he speaking with special emphasis? He drew her over to the cabinet where Rose Ducor had concealed a little shrine of the Madonna, opened it and laid down *le petit Roi de Gloire*. Then he began to pray. He prayed the *Regina coeli laetare*, the Easter greeting to the Mother of God.

I prayed too. In that hour I was like a child who drops through all the layers of being to the very foundation of all things which is a foundation everlasting because it belongs to God.—And now, my friend, it is your turn to speak!

In your warm eyes I seem to see two tears. They are falling on your grave hands. Your lips are closed, I might almost say, folded. You are moved but you are disquieted and I know why! You expected the victory of a heroine and you saw a miracle in one so weak!

But is it not this that kindles exceeding hope? The human element is not enough, not even when it is "admirably human", as we said so enthusiastically before the Revolution. (Ah! my friend, fundamentally this whole epoch teaches us only what we have already learned from poor little Blanche.) No, the purely human is not enough. It is not even enough to offer as a sacrifice. My friend, up to now the bond that existed between us included a union of ideas. Can you endure the change in your friend? Well—it is your turn!